Monster Camp!

'Monster Camp!'
An original concept by Kate Poels
© Kate Poels 2025

Illustrated by Vincent Batignole

Published by MAVERICK ARTS PUBLISHING LTD

Suite 1, Hillreed House, 54 Queen Street,

Horsham, West Sussex, RH13 5AD

© Maverick Arts Publishing Limited May 2025

+44 (0)1403 256941

A CIP catalogue record for this book is available at the British Library.

ISBN 978-1-83511-059-1

Printed in India

www.maverickbooks.co.uk

Monster Camp!

Written by
Kate Poels

Illustrated by
Vincent Batignole

Chapter 1
A Monster Trip

Every summer, several monsters of Froggington Academy are invited to take part in the **Mega Monster Camp Out.** This year, best friends Jiff, Spudly, Haggis and Vince were excited that it was finally their turn.

They filled their backpacks with snot-paste sandwiches, bottles of pondy-pop drink and pus gums to chew on as they walked.

Luckily, they also remembered their sleeping bags, fang brushes and clean pants.

Because it was a camping trip, they were given a tent to carry between them.

Haggis told them all a story about the fearsome Slugrotter who lived on the other side of the mountain.

"It has venomous fangs and razor-sharp claws," she said.

"And it likes to gobble up monsters for its tea," Jiff added.

Spudly shook in fright. He didn't like the stories and wanted them to stop, so he took out a can of fizzlewort spray.

"Hey," said Haggis. "Don't squirt that near me; it smells disgusting! **Peeyoow!**"

"But it keeps the bugs away," said Spudly.

"Put it away!" the other monsters shouted crossly.

Spudly put the fizzlewort spray away, but he smiled secretly because everyone had stopped talking about the Slugrotter.

"Which way do we need to go?" asked Jiff when they got to a split in the path. "Someone get the map out."

"I haven't got the map," all the monsters said at the same time. Then they looked at each other in dismay. How would they find the campsite now?

"I'm really good with directions," said Vince. "It's definitely this way. Come on."

They walked for a little way, chatting and laughing until a terrible noise made them stop in their tracks.

AARRGGH!

"Run!" shouted Jiff. "It sounds like the Slugrotter!"

The monsters ran and ran and didn't slow down until the noise was far behind them. They were frightened and nobody knew where they were. Something was strange about the ground in front of them. It looked almost like it was moving.

"Watch out!" shouted Haggis. "It looks like a sinky swamp."

Vince and Spudly stopped but it was too late for Jiff.

"Help me!" Jiff shouted as she started to sink into the mud.

"Quick!" yelled Spudly.

The monsters all held on to each other tightly.

"All pull together," said Spudly.

They started to pull and Jiff began to slowly slurp her way out of the gooey mud. But before she was free, there was another problem.

"Swamp boggles!" Haggis shouted.

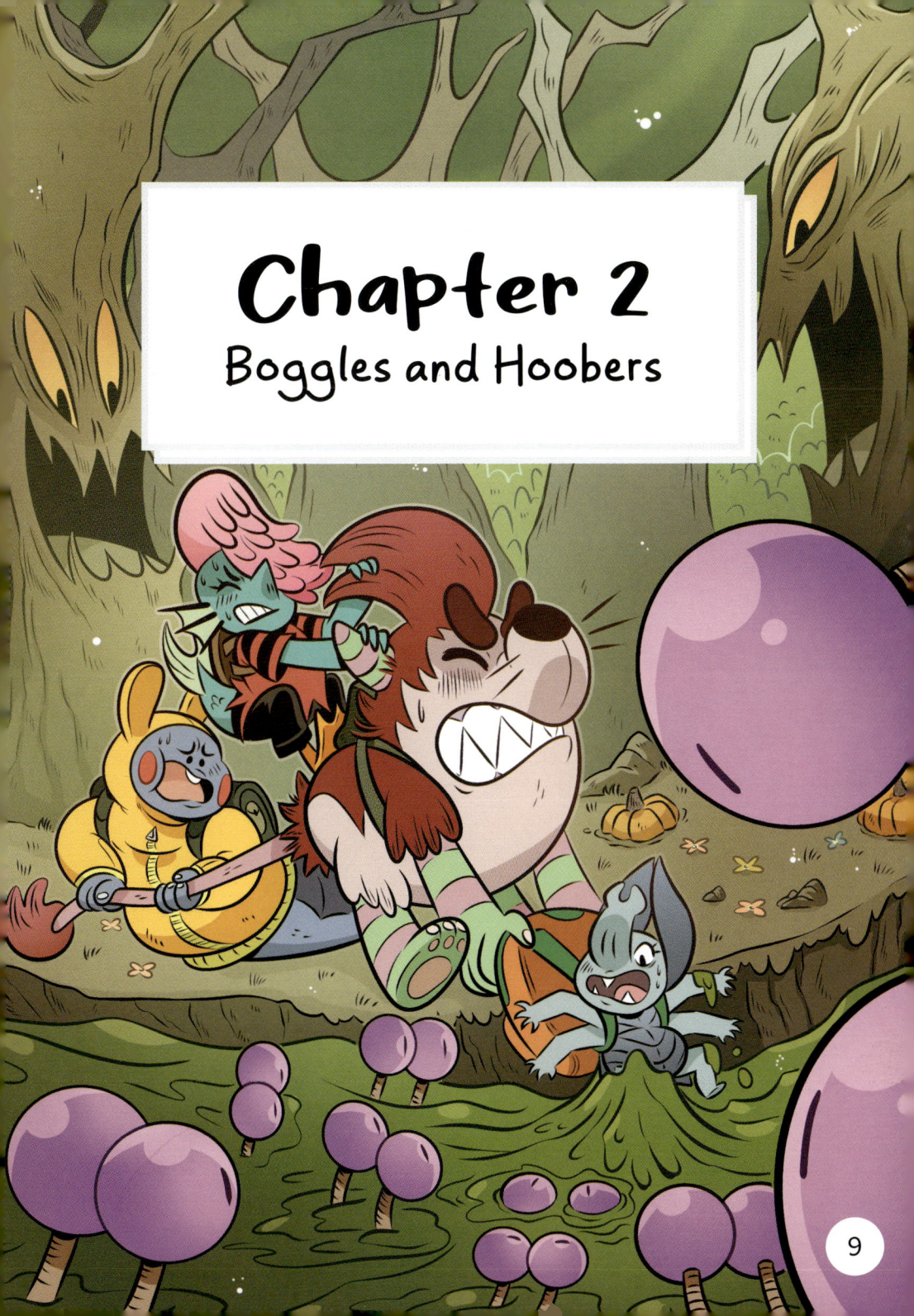

The fearsome sound of the Slugrotter rattled around the swamp, and the terrified friends wanted to run away.

"Boggles don't have ears!" cried Vince. "They can't hear the Slugrotter coming and they're not getting out of the way."

"If we don't escape soon, the Slugrotter will come and **eat us!**" shouted Haggis.

"Let's use our backpacks to help us push our way out!" yelled Jiff. "Quickly, hold hands and make a circle."

There was another roar; it sounded as though the Slugrotter was getting closer. They made a tight ring with their backpacks on the outside and then began to push.

"Heave!" shouted Jiff. "It's working!"

The boggles started to fall over as the monsters pushed against them until there was a big boggle pile on the ground.

Another loud roar ripped across the ground and the monsters wasted no more time. Soon, they'd left the boggles and the Slugrotter's roars behind them.

"Where do we go next?" Vince asked.

"I wish we had the map," said Spudly, trying not to cry.

The four friends were quiet and gloomy as they walked on. Even opening up a bag of yellow pus gums didn't make them feel any better.

They trudged on until they came to a place where four paths met at a crossroad. They stopped and looked around.

A monster with two heads and spiky hair jumped out from behind a tree, giving them all a fright.

"Are you lost?" one of the heads asked.

"We are," said Haggis as fat tears rolled down her face.

"Don't worry," said head number two. "We are a hoober, and hoobers are known for their excellent sense of direction."

"That's right," said head one. "Just tell us where you want to go."

The monsters felt their hearts lift. At last, they might be able to get to the campsite before the Slugrotter got to them.

"We are heading to the Mega Monster Camp Out," said Vince. "It's in Bugs Bottom field. Do you know it?"

"Of course!" said both heads at the same time.

Chapter 3
Attack of the Ripper-snippers

The monsters hurried off into the safety of the trees and walked deep into the woods, where they decided to stop for lunch as they were all tired and very hungry.

They sat on a log and opened their sandwiches.

"Do you think the Slugrotter will come into the forest?" asked Spudly.

"I hope not," said Vince. "It sounded really angry about something, and when I'm angry I always get hungry."

Spudly was so scared that he couldn't even eat his snot-paste sandwiches, so he packed them away again and waited for the others to finish theirs.

Suddenly, the air was filled with the flitter of little wings and a cloud of tiny ripper-snippers started to fly around their heads.

The monsters jumped to their feet and flapped their arms around to try and keep them away, but the annoying little insects kept coming. They landed on the sandwiches and tore off bits which they took up into the trees to enjoy.

"Get away!" the monsters shouted.

The ripper-snippers weren't bothered by the shouting or the hand waving. They just carried on buzzing around snipping and ripping whatever they could find.

"Not my T-shirt!" yelled Vince as lots of little holes appeared in all their clothes.

"Stay away from my bag!" shouted Haggis as the insects swarmed around in a big cloud.

Nothing that the monsters tried worked. There were too many ripper-snippers, and their teeth were tiny but incredibly sharp. When the monsters swatted at them, the insects bit back.

Chapter 4
Setting up a Monster Camp

Nobody said very much as they walked on.

The path was bumpy, and they kept stumbling and tripping.

"What's that noise?" Spudly said when there was a rustle in the bushes.

They all froze, waiting for the next scary creatures to jump out. But it was only a family of furry rabblings who paid them no attention as they scurried away down the path.

A little later on, there was a much larger crash somewhere behind them amongst the trees. It was definitely big enough to be the Slugrotter and it made the monsters speed up to try and stay well ahead.

The four monsters walked and walked until they came to a little clearing in the woods.

"It's getting late," said Haggis. "I don't think it's safe for us to go any further when it's already getting dark."

"But what about the Slugrotter?" Spudly asked.

"We haven't heard anything from it for ages," said Vince.

"Perhaps it's gone a different way," Jiff suggested.

"I can't take another step," said Haggis. "My feet are so sore. Let's pitch the tent and get some rest."

"Perhaps we will have better luck in the morning," said Jiff, "after we've had a good sleep."

"Alright then," said Spudly. "We'll put the tent up, but I don't think I will sleep a wink tonight knowing that we could be eaten up at any moment."

When they opened up their bags, a few stray ripper-snippers flew out. They weren't so brave when they didn't have the big swarm around them, and they flew off back into the forest.

"Help, it's the Slugrotter!"

The monsters scrambled around in the tent, trying to get out before the Slugrotter caught them all and ate them as a midnight snack.

The tent started to collapse around them, and they became tangled up in a jumble of poles and fabric.

"It's got my leg!" shouted Spudly.

"No it hasn't," said Vince. "You're stuck under my shoulder."

With a lot of wriggling, the four monsters managed to fight their way out of the ruined tent. They huddled together in the moonlight, staring around to see where the Slugrotter had gone.

"Do you think we scared it away?" Jiff asked.

"Don't be silly," said Haggis. "The Slugrotter isn't scared of anything."

"Well, where is it then?"

"Shh, listen," said Jiff.

Everything was eerily quiet.

They waited…

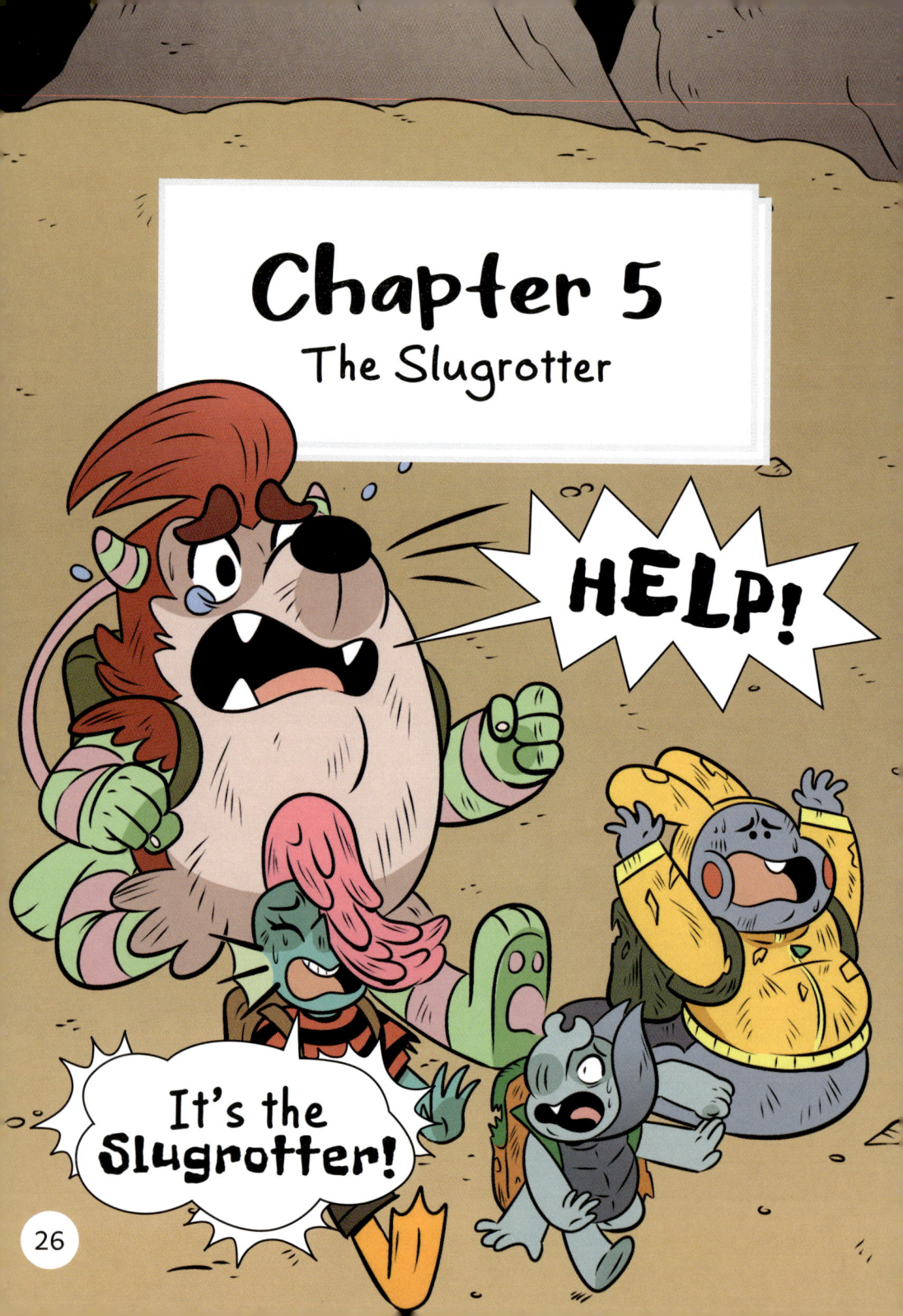

At the sight of the Slugrotter, everyone panicked. They tried to get away but fell over each other and landed in a heap.

A mighty howl from the Slugrotter made them panic even more as they tried to stumble to their feet.

"Stay away from us!" shouted Haggis. "If you don't then we will bash and crash and scream and shout."

Vince started to shout, but Spudly was too busy trying to hide himself behind a bush to join in.

It was little Jiff who was the first monster to notice that the Slugrotter didn't look as though he wanted to eat them.

"It looks scared of us," she said.

And she was right. The Slugrotter was cowering against a tree looking as frightened of them as they were of it.

"It can't be scared," said Vince. "It's been chasing us all day so that it can eat us for its dinner."

The Slugrotter looked shocked and shook its head quickly.

"You don't want to eat us?" Jiff asked.

It shook his head again.

"But you were roaring and howling," said Haggis.

The Slugrotter turned around and, in the light of the full moon, the monsters could see lots of long, spiky thorns sticking out of its bottom.

"It looks like you sat on a crackleberry bush," said Jiff.

The Slugrotter nodded sadly and waved its rather short arms in the air to show the monsters what the problem was.

"You can't reach to pull them out yourself," Haggis said.

The Slugrotter let out a sad groan.

"Would you like us to help you?" Jiff asked.

A big grin spread across the Slugrotter's face, and it clapped its hands together in delight.

"And you promise not to gobble us up?" said Spudly, coming out from his bush.

The Slugrotter nodded quickly and pretended to zip its lips together just to make sure they all knew it wasn't at all dangerous.

The monsters started to carefully pull the thorns out, and the Slugrotter tried not to scare them as it moaned and groaned in pain.

Walking back through the woods with the Slugrotter was so much fun, and they were soon at the edge of the woods.

"I can hear the others!" said Spudly. "And I can smell nettle and dandelion porridge cooking."

"I can't wait to tell everyone that we met the Slugrotter and that you were the one who helped us find the camp."

The Slugrotter shook his head quickly and looked scared at the very thought.

"What's the matter?" Vince asked.

"I think he's shy," said Jiff. "Do you like people thinking that you're scary so that it keeps them away?"

The Slugrotter nodded and gave them all a wave before he squelched off through the trees.

The monsters waved back and smiled. Then, they went to find their friends who were all sitting around the campfire.

"Where have you been?" everyone shouted.

"Well, let us tell you about our adventures with the scary, terrible, monster-guzzling Slugrotter!" said Haggis.

The End

WHAT NEXT?

Did you enjoy this Fusion Reader? If you are looking for more, the Maverick Reading Scheme is a bright, attractive range of books with plenty of stories for everyone.

MAVERICK FUSION READERS

To view the whole Maverick Reading Scheme, visit our website at www.maverickearlyreaders.com

Or scan the QR code to view our scheme instantly!